# Woven Reflections
## of
# Poems, Stories and Plays

# Woven Reflections
## of
## Poems, Stories and Plays

Ronok Ghosal
Rhea Ghosal

BLACK EAGLE BOOKS
Dublin, USA | Bhubaneswar, India

 Black Eagle Books
USA address:
7464 Wisdom Lane
Dublin, OH 43016

India address:
E/312, Trident Galaxy, Kalinga Nagar,
Bhubaneswar-751003, Odisha, India

E-mail: info@blackeaglebooks.org
Website: www.blackeaglebooks.org

First International Edition Published by
Black Eagle Books, 2025

**WOVEN REFLECTIONS OF POEMS, STORIES AND PLAYS**
by Ronok Ghosal | Rhea Ghosal

Cover & Interior Design: Ezy's Publication

ISBN- 978-1-64560-647-5 (Paperback)
Library of Congress Control Number: 2025931066

Printed in the United States of America

# Preface

This is a book of poems, stories, and plays. The texts that comprise this volume are a product of moments of our life: times looking back, times to search for, and times of change. However, these do not stand alone; they speak to each other within a layered experience unfolding across various formats.

We chose to begin with poetry because it captures a moment: the raw emotion, the flash of a thought often in the most distilled way. It can be a whisper, a shout, or a quiet realization that beckons the reader to interpret it in their own way. But sometimes, a moment needs more than that - it needs more context, more depth, and space to breathe.

That's where the short stories come into play, to be able to continue the themes developed in the poem and give a narrative slant to them. One will see the emergence of characters, and settings defined.

And then the plays. The way people talk, the spaces between, and the tension of what is never said have always interested us. Writing the stories into scripts seemed the natural step, allowing them to be articulated and performed and to live from the page. The transition from poetry to prose to stage was a way for me to experiment with perspective, structure, and voice.

For us, writing has always been about finding the right form to express an idea. Some thoughts are best left as poetry, others need to be lived through a story, and some are meant to be spoken out loud, felt in the rhythm of conversation. This book is a collection of those choices—a reflection of how words can shape and reshape meaning depending on how they are framed.

We hope you like reading this book as much as we did writing it.

**- Ronok and Rhea**

# Acknowledgments

We want to express our great thankfulness to Black Eagle Books, who believe in and support our work. Their excellent management and passion to work with us gave a face to this book.

We would also like to thank our parents for all their unconditional love, encouragement, and support. Your guidance and sacrifice mean a lot in this journey, and for everything that you both did, we are grateful forever.

**- Ronok and Rhea**

# Content

# The Lacquered Door

In a Brooklyn brownstone, a door stands tall
Beneath layers of Sherwin-Williams Gray Shingle,
Its wood, ancient oak, whispers through the hall
A silent keeper of secrets, every creak a signal.

Rusty hinges, singing in a low, mournful tone
A song of lives it has seen come and never last
Of laughter and sorrow, each deeply known
Echoes of an era not yet fully passed.

Through it walks a girl, clutching her Prada tote
Her heart heavy with dreams yet unspoken
The door's groans blend with her silent note
Of aspirations, she hopes to never be broken.

Lacquered surface, smooth as silk where she rests
Her gaze pale, white as the marrow of a bone
Connecting her wishes to the untold depths
Of everybody's desires, all except her own.

# Whispers Behind Gray Shingle

## *A Short Story Based on "The Lacquered Door"*

Settled within a brownstone of the bustling borough of Brooklyn, stood a door that had witnessed the resilience of mankind; through thick and thin, it remained firm in its place. Its exterior brought upon great endearment, for it was painted a dazzling hue of ashen gray, with a modern yet sophisticated look about it. Its meticulous, yet sturdy appearance gave way to the marvels of its very purpose–it was responsible for carrying the virtue of generations, and generations to come. The ancient oak was surely a door to be respected- not merely as a passage for entry, but as a preserver of the success and adaptability of man.

I often found myself at the entrance of the brownstone, marveling at the door's sturdy stature and elegant mannerism. Many dreamers came, and many passed the door, not caring to twist the knob. I was like those, until one day, sweet tragedies came echoing from the door, evoking a nonsensical eruption of phantoms that had turned to tormented souls over the wretched course of life. It was as if, somehow, the somber laments of the door held the key to rekindle the dreamer's tragic trajectory; my ears welcomed the pleasant sound. I felt a vague despondency overwhelming me and found myself incapable of turning away, incapable of unhearing the dreamers' wistful mourning. In spite of understanding very little of the true demeanor of the door, I felt drawn to its unsettling ambience. With a luxurious bag in my arms and aspirations held high in my heart, I pushed past the door and stepped inside, the door creaking shut behind.

The room it took me was a soothing brown feature, with tall ceilings that stretched to the skies above. Notable windows adorned the walls, allowing for wisps of sunshine to prance into the room from the partitions of thin-veiled curtains. It felt warmer in the room, and I was overcome with an intrinsic feeling of belonging. I carefully walked through the halls of the large room, feeling acquainted with the cozy atmosphere. The room became one of my dearest friends, but not dearer than the door that took me there. For every night, I would fall asleep to the door's soft lulls of crying dreamers.

My daily duties were made much easier with the well-humored and intelligent people of Brooklyn. For years, I enjoyed the routine task of calculating and welcoming; presenting and assisting fostered a sense of purpose to dwell in my heart. All the more, my tasks would bring upon favorable material and wealth, making me even more grateful for the benevolence Brooklyn. After my daily tasks, I would approach the familiar door and enter the room, surrendering myself to its subtle embrace. I stayed in it, listening to the strangled laments of the door until I had to wake up the next morning and repeat the dreadful cycle.

I thought happiness was guaranteed in this way of life, but was it only temporary satisfaction? Did I mistake the dignified years I spent serving others for joy? I often found myself roaming the dark streets of Brooklyn, aimlessly and dejected, in search of some sense of purpose. Even the pleasant faces of my delighted customers weren't enough to please me; I could sense their expressions momentarily flicker in an irrefutable lacquered sense. When I came back to the room, I now call my home, the door whispered the same songs- songs of the dreamers before me. They asked me if I could recall where I had buried my hopes and dreams. What did I gain from slaving away to nothingness, when my heart tingled for youthful joy under starry skies? I was damaged irrevocably when I realized there was no more aptitude for such a life. I felt that the door's laments seemed to resonate intimately with me. It was then that I noticed myself warping into the dreamers' songs and losing myself in such a lovely and injurious way. I had become a phantom- hidden and in search of lost dreams.

# Brooklyn Whispers

*A Short Play Based on "The Lacquered Door"*

**Characters:**
- **MAGDA** – A thirty-year-old fashion designer
- **MINDY** – Magda's assistant
- **WHISPERS** – Voices that echo from the door
- **CUSTOMER 1** – A customer in Magda's store
- **CUSTOMER 2** – A customer in Magda's store

**Setting:**
- A house in Brooklyn
- Magda's apartment
- The door acts as a recurrent motif throughout the play.

## Scene 1: The Door

*An elegant door nestled within the suburban parts of Brooklyn. Pedestrians walk past; the air filled with casual chatter. MAGDA stands in front of the door, nervous, carrying an expensive bag.*

**MAGDA** *(enters from left, contemplating)*

Such a sturdy and graceful appearance; I am curious about what it entails! How could one possibly turn their gaze from such wondrous sights to their own mundane businesses?

*Magda presses her ear to the door. Her eyes widen with surprise as WHISPERS begin to sing from the door.*

**WHISPERS** *(singing in harmony)*

In prospect of passion, you find here
Nothing more than blatant tunes

But worry not—
If I were an ordinary tradesman,
I would know not of
The light inside you
That once glistened gold
Is now reduced to that of a weak glim
That illuminates not even the idlest of hearts
So open me, and be not like others
Who dared to fervently beseech me
In hopes of themselves serving the world
In light of their own twittering pulse
And underwhelming graves

**MAGDA** (*clutching her luxurious bag*)
What can you see in me that I cannot? I do not understand you...but I am in desperate need of a promotion that yields success. Is the 'light' you speak of the same as what I am thinking? I pray you are able to lead me in the right direction...

*The whispers rise to a crescendo. In a daze, Magda twists the doorknob and enters the room.*

Scene 2: The Room
*Magda enters the room, which is warmly lit and inviting.*
**MAGDA**
How dazingly warm! I simply cannot believe I found myself such a wonderful place...I must make living arrangements now.
*She picks up a phone and dials a number. MINDY answers from the other side.*
**MINDY** (*over the phone*)
Good morning, ma'am.
**MAGDA**
Yes, good morning indeed! Mindy, I would like for you to

file the paperwork for my new house.

**MINDY**

Oh, what wonderful news! But…for how long are you planning on staying?

**MAGDA**

I believe good fortune and wealth is imminent in this house. I will stay until I have what was promised in the stars for me.

**MINDY** (to the audience)

Magda has always neglected rationality for the pursuit of success…it will become rather troublesome if this continues…however, it is her decision, and not mine.

Scene 3: Work

*Magda sits at her desk in a sleek, polished store. A theatrical spotlight hovers over her as she greets customers and works relentlessly. MINDY is seated next to her, working more slowly. Several CUSTOMERS enter, and the store fills with murmurs of conversation.*

**MAGDA** (warm, practiced voice)

Welcome! How can I assist you?

**CUSTOMER 1** (shoving a camera into her face)

I think we all would like to know if your invention will be beneficial to the world…the people want to know!

**MAGDA**

Ah, well you see…I guarantee we can replenish our generation with prosperity and good fortune! My invention–

*A crowd gathers around Magda, cheering and chanting her name.*

**CUSTOMER 2** (yelling)

You hear that, folks? We will all be saved from the wretched fate of poverty! Not one of us will ever die a

pauper!
*The scene fades as the crowd carries Magda in the air, cheers echoing.*

Scene 4: Magda's Apartment
*Magda gazes at the lacquered door of her apartment. Its architecture exudes old-world charm and modern-day sophistication. The door stands like a steadfast guardian, witnessing countless lives. Magda arrives from work, exhausted and dejected, and converses with the door.*

**MAGDA** *(disoriented, speaking to the door)*
How do you propose I go on? I can see my future, clear as day…bathed in gold and prosperity. But the more work I do, the more soulless I become, and the more my heart yearns for something out of reach. Will this feeling ever pass?

**WHISPERS**
Where have you buried your dreams?
This modest voice reasons with you
To not be blinded by monetary value
And forget the weakened heart
This modest voice reasons with you
Because my voice is but a symphony
Of those whose voices could not be heard
Because they were stifled by the plague
That stales the heart gray
And turns the soul numb

**MAGDA**
My company awaits me…the world is waiting for my success…so why do you chide me so? But I feel as if I must believe your warnings…you are wise beyond words. I will live a life of virtue and resilience, and not let foolishness be the subject of my story!

**MAGDA** *(talking to herself)*
Two summers and one winter ago, under the high ceiling of this room, I felt complete warmth. Since then, I have been entrapped in this illusion…
**MAGDA**
It's time to break free...

Scene 5: Brooklyn Street
*Magda takes a few deep breaths and gathers the courage to open the door.*
**MAGDA**
Yes, I disposed of it. I am not fit for this kind of a life. My eyes will now seek the warmth of passion, not the glittering of diamonds.
*Magda hums a mellow tune.*
**MAGDA**
My dreams have been restored!
*Curtain falls.*

**End of Play**

# Silk and Cedar

In Kyoto's ancient temple, beneath the vermillion gate,
I see cedar pillars rise, worn from the ages,
Draped in fabric, soft as a lover's weight,
Silk kimonos in hues of persimmon-torn-like pages.

Beneath the Torii, a monk kneels in prayer,
His breath mingling with the incense's smoky curl,
Echoes of ancestors linger in the air,
and The essence, and diverse energies swirl and whirl.

The cedar's scent, like Chanel No. 5, distinct and rare,
Merges with the silk's rustle, a delicate embrace,
I feel a dance of materials, an entrancing affair,
Binding the tangible to the spirit's grace.

In the evening light, shadows play on stone,
Forming patterns of the past, a silent lore,
My heart, like an untouched bone,
Finds peace in the timeless, forevermore.

# Atsuta Shrine - an abode of peace and hope

## A Short Story Based on "The Lacquered Door"

Atsuta Shrine, located in the heart of Kyoto, is an ancient temple where faith and hope are infused into souls steeped in the misery of mundane life. Etsuko, along with her father Haesung, frequently visited this temple as a child. Her favorite spot in the temple was the vermillion gate beneath which the cedar pillars rise. She was drawn to them and spent hours gazing at the worn-out engravings that had been done during the Meiji era.

Haesung used to narrate tales revolving around the temple's history to Etsuko. "It was Lady Acha, a nun who once had a vision in her dream which led to the building of Atsuta Shrine. You see her portrait there…" Draped in a silk kimono exuding hues of persimmon, torn pages depicted Lady Acha with a golden halo around her head, her eyes brimming with kindness. Etsuko was hypnotized by the angelic beauty and asked innumerable questions to her father regarding the portrait. Haesung patiently answered all her questions. Etsuko and her father's favorite destination was this shrine. Haesung never ran out of stories regarding the temple, and Etsuko was never tired of listening to those tales from the bygone era.

Years passed by. Etsuko is now a professor of history

at the University of Kyoto. She had done her research and completed her thesis on the origin of Atsuta Shrine, but over the years she lost her faith in anything divine. She now believed in artifacts more than oral narratives. The reason behind this might be the untimely departure of her father. No, Haesung didn't die; she was only fifteen years old when one morning her father couldn't be found. He abandoned his family and, like smoke, vanished into thin air. Those were hard times. During those days, Etsuko used to spend most hours of the day in bed, bitterly sobbing, praying to the Almighty to bring her father back while her mother, Fumiko, had to work overtime to aid her family and provide Etsuko with proper education. Ever since that morning, Etsuko never went near the vermillion gate of Atsuta Shrine.

However, no matter how hard one tries, the past can never be eluded. The History Department at the University of Kyoto planned an excursion to Atsuta Shrine, and Etsuko had to lead the group of students since this was her forte. Ten years later, Etsuko set foot on the shrine, and each step unraveled memories that intensified the void left by her father's absence. Kai, one of her students who adored her, asked her, "Ma'am, please tell us something about the vermillion Torii gate." Etsuko was about to narrate all those tales when her eyes fell on a monk knelt in prayer, his breath blending seamlessly with the spiraling smoke from incense sticks. She asked her students to observe this scene and feel the diverse energies that were swirling and whirling. None of them uttered a word, and through their silence, they unknowingly paid homage to those ancestors whose sacrifice and resilience turned this place into an empyrean shrine.

When Etsuko started narrating the stories of Atsuta

Shrine, it was a cathartic moment for her. Her repressed emotions flowed through her words. The cedar's scent reminisced of Chanel No. 5, her father's favorite perfume and the one he wore most of the time. She coincidentally wore the same perfume that day. The smell merging with the silk of her kimono embraced her; it was an entrancing affair between her past and present. Etsuko saw a glimpse of her father, felt his touch through the embrace, but was again pulled back to reality.

"So, where was I, students? Alright, I hope I answered all of your questions." It was almost evening when she finished her lecture. Seeing the shadows playing on the stone, she realized that somewhere in this play of light and darkness, there's something sublime that is inexpressible and can only be felt. There are silent lores wrapped in every stone, and by touching one of the stones, Etsuko recalled those times when she used to be awestruck looking at the portrait of Lady Acha. She sighed for not being able to share this moment with her father, but her brief surreal encounter with her long-lost father that day rekindled her faith in divinity. She would forever treasure this moment in her heart and carry it to her grave. After decades, she finally felt at peace confronting her emotions and hoped that beyond this tangible world, in the spiritual realm, someday she would reunite with her father.

# Timeless Threads

## *A Short Play Based on "Silk and Cedar"*

**Characters:**

- **ETSUKO** – A young professor of History at the University of Kyoto
- **HAESUNG** – Etsuko's father who one fine day deserted his family
- **FUMIKO** – Etsuko's mother
- **KAI** – Etsuko's student
- **HISAO KIBUNE** – A senior professor and the Head of the History Department at the University of Kyoto

**Setting:**

- **Atsuta Shrine**
- **Etsuko's Home**
- **University of Kyoto**
- *The vermillion Torii gate* acts as a bridge between Etsuko's past and present.

Scene 1: Beneath the Vermillion Gate

*Soft-focused lights illuminate the **vermillion gate** placed at center stage. The cedar pillars and Lady Acha's portrait are visible inside. A harmonious sound is played by the Koto.*
***HAESUNG** and **ETSUKO** enter the stage from left.*

**ETSUKO**

*(asking her father)*

Dad, I want to know more about the Atsuta Shrine. Please, tell me more stories.

*Etsuko gazes at the worn-out engravings on the cedar pillar.*

**HAESUNG**

*(talking to Etsuko)*

You know, Etsuko, this shrine was built during the Meiji era.

*Etsuko listens carefully to her father's stories.*

**HAESUNG**

Have you heard of Lady Acha?

**ETSUKO**

No, Dad. Tell me about her.

**HAESUNG**

Lady Acha was a nun who once had a vision in her dream, which led to the building of Atsuta Shrine. You see her portrait there...

*Draped in a silk kimono exuding hues of persimmon, torn pages depict Lady Acha with a golden halo around her head, her eyes brimming with kindness. Etsuko is hypnotized by her angelic beauty.*

**HAESUNG**

*(continuing)*

Lady Acha's vision inspired the creation of this sacred place. Her legacy lives on in every stone and every prayer offered here.


Scene 2: Etsuko's Home

*10 Years Later*

*Focus lights fall on **Etsuko's bed** placed at center stage. Etsuko is bitterly sobbing and praying feverishly.*

**FUMIKO**

*(reprimanding Etsuko)*

How long are you going to lay in bed? Get up and get ready for school.

**ETSUKO**

*(blabbering)*

Dad, please come back!! Dad, where are you... Dad!

*Etsuko continues blabbering until her mother reprimands her again.*

**FUMIKO**

*(frustrated)*

I am working day and night for your sake, and you are not respecting my hard work. Your father is not going to be back.

*Etsuko sobs bitterly, repeating the same words.*

**ETSUKO**

*(monologue)*

Mom, don't be so harsh on me...I beg you... have some faith... he will be back...

*Etsuko prays feverishly to the Almighty to bring her father back.*


Scene 3: University of Kyoto

*Another 15 Years Later*

*A mellow light falls on* **Etsuko**, *now a Professor of History at the University of Kyoto. She is doing some paperwork at her desk placed at center stage.* **HISAO KIBUNE** *enters the stage from left.*

**HISAO KIBUNE**

*(smiling warmly and greeting)*

Hello, Etsuko! Am I interrupting your important work?

**ETSUKO**

*(smiling back and greeting)*

Hello, sir! Absolutely not. Please, tell me how I can help you.

**HISAO KIBUNE**

Etsuko, I was planning an excursion for the students of our department, and after prolonged contemplation,

I decided that Atsuta Shrine will be the best place—a significant part of Japanese history. Moreover, your thesis is on the origin of this shrine, so this is your forte. You will be leading the group of students.

**ETSUKO**

*(hesitant and thoughtful)*

But, sir… I mean… I will let you know.

**HISAO KIBUNE**

Etsuko, there's no one better than you for this work. I request you to shoulder this responsibility.

*Etsuko hesitantly nods her head in approval.*

Scene 4: Atsuta Shrine

*The lights shift to a soft, mellow glow with a golden focus falling on **Etsuko** entering the shrine. Every step stirs memories as her students follow her.*

**KAI**

*(curious)*

Ma'am, please tell us something about the vermillion Torii gate.

**ETSUKO**

I will. Before that, look at the monk over there, knelt in prayer. Observe carefully how his breath blends seamlessly with the smoke spiraling from the incense sticks.

**KAI**

Ma'am, so we can deduce from here that history has some traces of divinity. It's not just artifacts.

**ETSUKO**

Shush! Feel the diverse energies that are swirling and whirling. You all know these energies are echoes of those ancestors whose sacrifice and resilience turned this place into an empyrean shrine.

*The students are almost hypnotized by the serene atmosphere, imploring Etsuko to now take them near the vermillion gate.*

Scene 5: Beneath the Vermillion Gate
*The **vermillion gate** is again placed at the center of the stage. **Etsuko** and her students enter the stage from right.*
**ETSUKO**
*(with a heavy heart)*
Students, this was my favorite spot in the entire temple. I visited this place frequently with my father...
*She stops midway, smelling a cedar scent.*
*The cedar's scent reminds her of Chanel No. 5, her father's favorite perfume and the one he wore most of the time. She coincidentally wears the same perfume that day. The smell merges with the silk of her kimono, embracing her in an entrancing affair between her past and present. Etsuko sees a glimpse of her father and feels his touch through the embrace but is again pulled back to reality.*
*A golden focus light falls on Etsuko.*
**KAI**
*(curious)*
Ma'am, are you alright? You have been standing like a statue without a word for almost ten minutes now. I thought you were going to ask us to observe something again. Are you alright, ma'am?
*Etsuko awakens from her reverie by a sudden jerk.*
**ETSUKO**
My apologies, students. I got lost in my thoughts. This place is very close to my heart... Lady Acha....
*Etsuko narrates the tales she heard from her father during childhood.*

Scene 6: Beyond the Tangible

*Rose pink lights are used to create the effect of twilight. **Atsuta Shrine** is placed at the center of the stage. **Etsuko** observes the evening light casting long shadows on the stones, forming patterns of the past. A silent lore is wrapped in every stone.*

**ETSUKO**

*(talking to herself)*

In this play of light and darkness, there's something sublime that is inexpressible and can only be felt... I shall forever treasure that moment and carry it to my grave.

*After decades, Etsuko finally feels at peace, confronting her emotions. She hopes that beyond this tangible world, in the spiritual realm, someday she will reunite with her father.*

**End of Play**

# Neon Dreams

On Tokyo's bustling Shibuya streets,
Neon lights flicker, like gas stove flames,
Gucci sneakers tread where the heartbeat meets,
Concrete and dreams, in fleeting lanes.

Billboards flash, in vibrant hues,
Of crimson, sapphire, and jade,
A canvas of stories, of gains and blues,
Where reality and fantasy seamlessly wade.

A barista at Starbucks, latte art in hand,
Crafts a heart in frothy white,
Connecting with a customer, a silent band,
Of shared warmth in the city's night.

The aroma of coffee, rich and deep,
Blends with the scent of rain on asphalt,
Creating a locket, for memories to keep,
Where the tangible and intangible exalt.

In the neon glow, faces blur and blend,
Strangers and friends in a dance unseen,
A city's pulse, a connection to mend,
In the quiet, where lost hopes.

# Evanescent Connections

### *A Short Story Based on "Neon Dreams"*

Kazuo had migrated from Hiroshima to Tokyo with dreams of becoming a film director. It had been five years since Kazuo's debut film was released, but ever since then, he hadn't been able to make any new films. The producers had given up on him after imploring him to devise ideas and plans, but Kazuo felt disoriented. His quest to find a muse turned futile every time.

Burdened by his deferred dreams, one day he was walking through the bustling Shibuya streets when the neon lights caught his attention. They flickered like gas stove flames, reflecting the phantasmagoria of urban life. Gucci sneakers fleeting like racing heartbeats. Opulence and vehemence met at the concrete, creating a disjunctured harmony echoing his beaten dreams.

As Kazuo navigated through the streets, he came across a photographer passionately capturing the billboards flashing in vibrant hues of crimson, sapphire, and jade. After exchanging a few conversations, Kazuo discovered that the photographer hailed from his hometown. Kenji was the name of the photographer who chose Tokyo for his project titled "Cityscapes."

"Why did you choose Tokyo?" asked Kazuo.

"Well, every month, thousands of people migrate to Tokyo in the quest for their dreams. In the process of chasing their dreams, most of them lose and loathe themselves, trapped in the pangs of urbanity. These billboards you see carry a canvas of stories reflecting the zenith and nadir of time. The photographs you see wade reality and fantasy seamlessly," Kenji explained.

Following his enlightening conversation with the photographer, Kazuo felt that maybe his search for a muse was finally narrowing down.

Like a flaneur crossing different alleys of Shibuya streets, Kazuo had an epiphany while observing a barista at Starbucks. Her pensive eyes overflowed with passion for latte art. She was crafting a heart in frothy white foam. "Heart so fragile, yet everyone preserves it… treasures it," Kazuo mumbled to himself.

The soft warm lights glowing through the window prompted Kazuo to go inside. He pushed open the door and was immediately drawn to a quote inscribed on one of the walls, highlighted in neon yellow lights: "Home is where the heart is." The aroma of brewing coffee stirred memories of a rainy night, one of the darkest nights of Kazuo's life. That night, he had tried hard to give up on life. The asphalt streets stood as witnesses to several fading faces and fleeting steps.

"I desired to fade away that night in the dark… in the rain… but I couldn't because there was this tune, oh, I cannot remember… It drew me towards it… intoxicated me and made me fall asleep," Kazuo once again mumbled to himself.

"Sir, shall I note your order?" asked the barista.

"Well, a cappuccino only… what's your name?" replied Kazuo.

Through their conversation, he discovered that the barista was an artist, but due to circumstantial adversities, she had to work in a café. However, she channelized her passion for art through latte art. Kazuo realized that he was fortunate enough to pursue his passion when he was greeted by a familiar face—Emiko, the actress from his debut film.

"Kazuo, how's your new project coming along?" Emiko asked.

Kazuo was embarrassed but replied that he was still figuring it out. Meeting his friend after ages, he confided in her, releasing the burden of his stress—how he still searched for a home in this city and how the city stripped him of his creativity, ensnaring him in its banal urbanity.

"Sometimes in life, we might feel lost, but the best we can do is to embrace the chaos and make something out of what we have," said Emiko.

While Kazuo sipped his cappuccino, his eyes brimmed with newfound clarity as he looked outside the window where the faces of strangers and friends blurred and blended in the neon glow. He heard the same tune that lulled him to sleep that night. "Palpable city pulse and ephemeral connections," he mumbled to himself.

"Yes sir, you are right... we are all God's lonely children in some way or another," replied the barista. Kazuo smiled awkwardly, appreciating her gesture.

The sky grew dark, and soon it started to pour. As Kazuo strode through the asphalt streets again, drenched in rain, the neon lights cast a kaleidoscope of colors onto the rain-slicked sidewalks. He was no longer at sea since he had finally found the muse for his new project.

"Art and chaos indeed go hand in hand... just like Shibuya streets and the evanescent dreams and connections of its passers-by," muttered Kazuo.

# Neon Muse

### A Short Play Based on "Neon Dreams"

Characters:
- **KAZUO** – A young filmmaker undergoing a creative block
- **KENJI** – A photographer
- **ETSUKO** – A barista with a passion for latte art
- **EMIKO** – Kazuo's friend and the actress from his debut film

Setting:
- **Bustling Shibuya Street**
- **Starbucks Café**
- *Neon lights* act as a recurrent motif in the play. The play transitions between vibrant streets and the café interior.

Scene 1: Shibuya Street
*Neon lights illuminate the **Shibuya Street**, placed at center stage.*
**KAZUO**
*(loitering around, disoriented)*
How long will it take me to find my muse? I feel helpless. *Burdened by his deferred dreams, Kazuo walks through the bustling Shibuya streets. The neon lights flicker like gas stove flames, reflecting the phantasmagoria of urban life.*
**KENJI**
*(astonished)*
Gucci sneakers fleeting like racing heartbeats. Concrete

and dreams in fleeting lanes. This city is devouring me.
*Kazuo navigates through the streets and comes across KENJI,*
*the photographer.*
**KAZUO**
*(warmly greeting)*
Hello!! What are you capturing? I am Kazuo, by the way.
**KENJI**
*(warmly greeting back)*
Hello!! I am capturing these billboards flashing in vibrant
hues of crimson, sapphire, and jade for my upcoming
project titled "Cityscapes."
**KAZUO**
*(curious)*
Why did you choose Tokyo?
**KENJI**
*(monologue)*
Well, every month, thousands of people migrate to Tokyo
in the quest for their dreams. In the process of chasing
their dreams, most of them lose and loathe themselves,
trapped in the pangs of urbanity. These billboards you see
carry a canvas of stories reflecting the zenith and nadir of
time. The photographs you see wade reality and fantasy
seamlessly.
*Following his enlightening conversation with the photographer,*
*Kazuo feels that maybe his search for a muse is finally*
*narrowing down.*

Scene 2: Epiphany at Starbucks
*Warm focus lights fall on **ETSUKO**, the barista. **KAZUO***
*enters the stage from left.*
**KAZUO**
*(in wonder, observing the barista)*
Her eyes are filled with passion for her latte art... Oh!!

She is crafting a heart in the frothy white foam. A heart so fragile... yet everyone preserves it... treasures it.

*The soft warm lights glow through the window of the café, prompting Kazuo to go inside. He pushes open the door and undergoes an epiphany when he sees a quote inscribed on one of the walls, highlighted in neon yellow lights: "Home is where the heart is."*

**KAZUO**
*(monologue)*
The aroma of brewing coffee stirs my memories of a rainy night, one of the darkest nights of my life. I desired to fade away that night in the dark... in the rain... but I couldn't because there was this tune, oh, I cannot remember... It drew me towards it... intoxicated me and made me fall asleep.

**ETSUKO**
Sir, shall I note your order?

**KAZUO**
Well, a cappuccino only... What's your name?

**ETSUKO**
I am Etsuko, sir.

**KAZUO**
You are such a passionate artist. I can see it through your latte art. Why are you working here?

**ETSUKO**
I am an artist, but due to circumstantial adversities, I have to work in this café. I channelize my passion for art through latte art.

*Kazuo realizes that he is fortunate enough to pursue his passion.*

Scene 3: Reunion with a Friend at Starbucks
*Lights focus on the **Starbucks Café interior**, placed at center stage. Lights on the exterior shift to the **Shibuya Street**.*

*EMIKO enters the stage from left.*
**EMIKO**
*(warmly greeting)*
Hi Kazuo, long time no see. How are you doing?
**KAZUO**
*(smiling warmly)*
Hey Emiko, yes, I am doing fine.
**EMIKO**
*(curious)*
How's your new project coming along?
**KAZUO**
*(embarrassed)*
Still figuring out.
*A few minutes of silence.*
**KAZUO**
*(monologue)*
You know, Emiko, I am still searching for a home in this city. This city has stripped me of my creativity. I have nowhere to go, nothing makes sense to me anymore.
**EMIKO**
*(consoling and advising)*
Sometimes in life, we may feel lost, but the best we can do is to embrace the chaos and make something out of it.
*Emiko's words help Kazuo find a new perspective.*

Scene 4: Reflections on Life
*Soft warm lights fall on **ETSUKO**, the barista. Focus lights are fixed on **KAZUO** sipping his cappuccino, his eyes brimming with newfound clarity.*
**KAZUO**
*(looking outside the window)*
Oh, how the faces of strangers and friends blur and blend in the neon glow... the palpable city pulse and ephemeral

connections.

**ETSUKO**

Yes, sir, you are right... We are all God's lonely children in some way or another.

*Kazuo smiles awkwardly, appreciating her gesture.*

Scene 5: Shibuya Street and New Muse

*Dark lights depict a cloudy sky. The neon lights cast a kaleidoscope of colors onto the rain-slicked sidewalks.*

**KAZUO**

*(drenched in rain, mumbling to himself)*

I am no longer at sea... I've finally found my new muse for my new project... Art and chaos indeed go hand in hand... just like the evanescent dreams and connections of the passers-by on Shibuya streets...

**End of Play**

# Reflecting on Reflections

In the mirror's glow, I see a face askew,
A jigsaw puzzle in a soup of stars,
I wonder what the next odd step might do.
Should I step out or bake a pie of glue?

The world outside is never quite as far,
In the mirror's glow, I see a face askew.
A calendar of socks, in colors new,
Spins slowly while my thoughts are stuck in jars,

I wonder what the next odd step might do.
I dream of sailing boats on rivers blue,
Yet find my anchor's tangled in bizarre,
In the mirror's glow, I see a face askew.

A symphony of shadows plays askew,
While apathy's a ship with rusty bars,
I wonder what the next odd step might do.
I'm tangled in a web of things I knew,

Yet paralyzed by ghosts of things afar,
In the mirror's glow,
I see a face askew,
I wonder what the next odd step might do.

# Untangled Reflections

*A Short Story Based on "Reflecting on Reflections"*

The walls of her apartment were painted in grey. The windows were slightly ajar, and streaks of light fell on the crumbled bedsheets. Kelly stood in front of her full-length mirror. In the mirror's golden glow, she saw a face askew.

"Hi, I am Nelly. You know me, right? We have been friends for a while now."

Kelly's gaze turned pale and translucent. Her life seemed like a jigsaw puzzle, while on the contrary, she felt like she was walking in a galaxy of stars, each star signifying her dreams that were gradually losing their shine.

Kelly's apartment was in the heart of New York City, the city that never sleeps and never lets her sleep. It had been months since sleep hadn't knocked on Kelly's weary eyes. Her eyeballs seemed to be oozing out of the sockets. In this riddle called life, the lines between dreams and reality had been blurred.

"Should I step out or bake a pie of glue?" Such hogwash questions kept bothering Kelly. Her life lately was a chaotic soup of conflicting thoughts. The more she tried to make sense of it, the more she felt lost in the maze.

She stood still, looking at the mirror, examining the bags under her eyes. Her fragile limbs hung loosely by her side, and a voice constantly echoed in her mind.

"Hi, I am Nelly. Look at the calendar of socks... such vibrant landscapes on each page... time is slipping by, Kelly... and you are stuck in this jar of thoughts... break free."

Kelly was swimming in a mayhem of numerous hallucinations. Her neurosis intensified with every voice playing in her mind.

Kelly desired to be a sailor who sailed ships on river blue. She wanted to be a traveler who would conquer the world, but the anchor of her ship was rusty and tangled in bizarre circumstances.

"What's this neurosis... who is Nelly... this writhing pain devouring me... I want to sleep."

As evening broke and a symphony of shadows played askew, Kelly still found herself standing in front of the mirror, her legs almost numb. Kelly was a writer who migrated to New York for her new job at a publishing house. However, due to some misunderstandings and unfortunate circumstances, she lost her job. One more American dream crumbled. It's hard to survive in such an expensive city, especially when one's unemployed.

However, Kelly didn't give up. She tried her luck in other professions such as that of a tour guide, but someone more able and efficient replaced her soon in that field. Kelly was heartbroken; she felt as if the city had cursed her fate. But such is life.

A hyperactive and overenthusiastic Kelly barely talked now. She turned into a vegetable who talked only to her reflection.

"Hi, I am Nelly... Kelly, will you come to my world... if you want to... then hold my hand..."

Kelly's face slowly turned askew, her jaws widened, she was smiling, and tears were rolling down her cheeks at the same time.

"What's happening to me... I can't see anything... this writhing pain..."

There was a blackout, and when Kelly opened her eyes, she found herself in the bed of a hospital.

"How are you feeling, Miss Kelly Murphy?" asked the doctor.

"I am feeling much better, doctor... what happened to me?"

The doctor replied that she had been unconscious for a while and that when her neighbor Steve knocked on her door and didn't get any response, he broke open the door and found her lying on the floor.

"You must rest now. You had an anxiety attack, Miss Kelly. Do you want to share what's bothering you?"

Kelly said that she had developed an apathy towards life as she was tangled in a web of things.

"The ghosts of things afar paralyzed me. Innumerable times, I heard the voice of a girl named Nelly... I don't know who she was... but she looked exactly like me."

The doctor instructed Kelly to keep calm and lie down still in bed.

"It's just a rough patch of time, Miss Kelly. Hold still."

"I'm trying my best, doctor."

"Keep trying, and no worries, I am here to help you."

As Kelly lay in bed, she touched her face with her hands. Her face wasn't askew anymore; it had straightened up.

"I guess it was just my overthinking strangling me. I feel so much better now."

Kelly was engrossed in deep contemplation when her jaws dropped listening to a familiar voice.

"Hi, Kelly. I am Nelly... welcome to my world... I told you... you are going to feel better here."

"Who are you? What do you want from me?" asked Kelly in a shaky voice.

"Well, I am you, Kelly, and I want you," replied the voice, laughing hysterically.

# Mirror's Voice

### A Short Play on "Reflecting on Reflections"

**Characters:**
- **KELLY** – A writer who's undergoing a neurosis
- **NELLY/VOICE OF THE MIRROR** – Alter ego of Kelly/ inner voice
- **STEVE** – Kelly's neighbor
- **DOCTOR** – The person who's treating Kelly

**Setting:**
- **A dimly lit bedroom** with grey walls and a large ornate mirror standing against one wall
- **Doctor's chamber**
- *The mirror and its reflection* throughout the play act as symbols of Kelly's emotional burden and beaten dreams

Scene 1: Reflections

*Lights up on* **KELLY**, *who is gazing at the ornate mirror. Soft lights fall on the crumbled bedsheets of her bed. The mirror is placed at the center stage.*

**KELLY**

*(talking to her reflection)*

This face askew is looking like a jigsaw puzzle in a soup of stars, not making any sense, just like my life.

**VOICE OF THE MIRROR (NELLY)**

Hi, I am Nelly. You know me, right? We have been friends for a while now.

**KELLY**

*(confused)*

We know each other? No, I don't remember knowing you.

**NELLY**

Don't you remember those nights of our endless conversations when you asked if you should step out or bake a pie of glue?

**KELLY**

*(startled)*

A pie of glue... this phrase sounds familiar, but I don't remember.

**NELLY**

That's because you're swimming in a chaotic soup of conflicting thoughts. Look at the calendar of socks... such vibrant landscapes on each page... time is slipping by, Kelly... and you are stuck in this jar of thoughts... break free.

**KELLY**

*(mumbling)*

I feel like treading in a galaxy of stars only to discover that each star is losing its shine.

**NELLY**

Those are your dreams, Kelly. Your crumbled American dreams. Oh, I remember you telling me how you wanted to be a writer...

**KELLY**

Well, I want to be a sailor who sails ships on river blue. I desire adventure, but my ship's rusty anchor is tangled in bizarre.

**NELLY**

No, that's not bizarre. Your fate is bizarre. New York City cursed your fate.

*Kelly's gaze turns pale. Her fragile limbs hang loosely by her side. Her eyeballs ooze out of their sockets. Sleep hasn't visited*

*Kelly's eyes for a long time, but she continues to gaze at the mirror.*

## Scene 2: Nemesis

*Lights remain on **KELLY**, but they have been dimmed to some extent. A symphony of shadows plays askew.*

**KELLY**

What's this neurosis... who is Nelly... this writhing pain devouring me... I want to sleep.

**NELLY**

*(warmly)*

Hi, Kelly. Will you come to my world... if you want to... then hold my hand...

**KELLY**

*(astonished)*

Is your world better than mine? Will I be free there?

**NELLY**

*(assuring)*

Hold my hand, dear... hold my hand...

**STEVE**

*(gently knocking on Kelly's door)*

Hello, Kel... you... there... I want to talk to you.

**KELLY**

*(distressed)*

My face turning askew, my jaws widening, forcing my lips to curve up into a smile, tears rolling down my cheeks... I can't see anything... oh, this writhing pain.

**STEVE**

*(worried)*

Kelly... where are you? Please open the door. I think there's something wrong.

*There's a blackout. When Kelly opens her eyes, she finds herself lying on a hospital bed.*

## Scene 3: Doctor's Chamber

*Focus lights fall on both* **DOCTOR** *and* **KELLY**, *her bed placed at the center of the stage.*

**DOCTOR**

How are you feeling, Miss Kelly Murphy?

**KELLY**

I am feeling much better, doctor... what happened to me?

**DOCTOR**

Well, your neighbor Steve was knocking on your door. After not getting any response, he broke open the door and found you lying unconscious on the floor.

**KELLY**

Where's Steve?

**DOCTOR**

Well, he's waiting outside. You must rest now. You had an anxiety attack, Miss Kelly. Would you mind sharing what's bothering you?

**KELLY**

*(monologue)*

I have developed a sudden apathy towards life as I am tangled in a web of things. The ghosts of things afar paralyze me. Innumerable times, I have heard the voice of a girl named Nelly... I don't know who she is... but she looks exactly like me.

**DOCTOR**

Keep calm and lie down still in bed. It's just a rough patch of time, Miss Kelly. Hold still.

**KELLY**

I am trying my best, doctor.

**DOCTOR**

Keep trying, and no worries, I am here to help you.

*Lying still in bed, Kelly touches her face with her hands. Her face isn't askew anymore; it has straightened up.*

**KELLY**

I guess it was just my overthinking that strangled me. I feel so much better now.

*The voice of the mirror returns.*

**VOICE OF THE MIRROR (NELLY)**

Hi, Kelly. I am Nelly... welcome to my world... I told you... you are going to feel better here.

**KELLY**

*(shaky voice)*

Who are you? What do you want from me?

**NELLY**

*(laughing hysterically)*

Well, I am you, Kelly, and I want you…

**End of Play**

# Grains and Seeds

On the edge where moments get tangled,
Bits of reality scatter like spilled seeds,
The rhythm of seasons churns with wild unpredictability,
Sunsets blend into the horizon's endless canvas.

Each wave hits, snatching away remnants,
Erasing paths of once-steadfast hopes,
In their absence, a complex pattern forms,
The relentless ebb of days, a puzzle to piece together.

As the sand gets swallowed by the tides,
New traces emerge from the churn of life,
In the void of what's lost, subtle connections appear,
As grains dissolve, they signal fresh beginnings.

Unmet aspirations float through shifting currents,
Time, a kaleidoscope of change, redefines everything.

# Tides of Change

## *A Short Story Based on "Grains and Seeds"*

L ately, Gelsomina felt at sea; her whole world seemed to be falling apart. She was on the edge of giving up her life, each moment of her existence tangled up in bits of harsh reality that scattered like spilled seeds—seeds that also pierced her conscience when she looked at Selena, her ten-year-old daughter.

"Momma, why are you crying? Please don't cry, Momma… I will be a good girl," Selena said, wiping her mom's tears.

It had been just a year since Selena lost her father, Gelsomina—the only love of her life. Life had been hard after Adam's untimely demise. Gelsomina had to switch jobs, manage her house, and care for her daughter; shouldering all these responsibilities gave her very little time to do what she loved most: painting. As the rhythm of the seasons unfolded, it only brought uncertainty and unpredictability, intensifying Gelsomina's woe. Watching sunsets blend into the horizon's endless canvas, Gelsomina desired the warmth she used to feel in Adam's arms. Life was beautiful and each moment fulfilling in Adam's presence, but it turned drab in the blink of an eye. The void of a loved one's absence could be really excruciating; therefore, Gelsomina planned to take a few days off and take a trip to a beach that was an abode of many fond memories. She hoped that maybe a change of place for a few days would be good for both her and her daughter.

Brighton Beach was their holiday destination for a week. "Momma, would you be making sandcastles with me? And would we be going scuba diving?" Gelsomina nodded her head in approval. This was the very beach where Adam had proposed to Gelsomina for the first time, which gradually led to their marriage. Gelsomina chose this place to scatter his ashes so that they could bid Adam a proper goodbye. With each wave hitting the shore and snatching away the remnants of the past, Gelsomina realized how the paths of one's steadfast hopes are erased by the ebb and flow of tides.

"Such is life—it's hard and complex, but we have to go on, enduring the relentless ebb of days, searching for the missing pieces of our jigsaw puzzle," Gelsomina mumbled to herself.

"Momma, look! The tides are swallowing the sands. Can you paint this? It's such a beautiful sight. You know, Dada once told me when the grains of sand dissolve in the sea, they signal new beginnings," said Selena.

"Yes, new traces emerge from the churn of life. In the void of what's lost, subtle connections appear," sighed Gelsomina.

Selena exclaimed in wonder, "I don't understand what you mean. This is sheer poetic language… you're talking like Dada."

"You will understand the meaning of this in due time," replied Gelsomina, smiling warmly.

"Without any further ado, let's now scatter Dada—aka Adam's ashes—and let's pray for his happiness and well-being," said Gelsomina in a shaky voice, tears rolling down her cheeks.

"Momma, don't cry…. Dada would be sad to see you crying…," said Selena, wiping Gelsomina's tears.

Gelsomina was astonished by her daughter's strength and resilience. "You got this from your father—staying positive all the time, being calm and fearless in the face of any danger," said Gelsomina.

"Well, now that Dada's afar, you have me, Momma… Can we build sandcastles now…," exclaimed Selena in excitement.

Gelsomina and Selena did everything they had planned on doing on this trip. As Gelsomina gazed at the sea, the sunset blending into the horizon, she didn't feel mad anymore… rather, she felt calm. She finally managed to let go of the burden that made her heart heavy. The tidal currents, glazed in crimson hues of sunset, echoed her unmet aspirations. She decided to start painting again as it was her escape from this tangible world—it was her medium of expression. The trip really gifted both Gelsomina and her daughter a rewarding experience, especially Gelsomina, who finally perceived that time is a kaleidoscope of change and that everything or everyone is temporal or temporary in this mortal world. Only death and change are constant, and it's change that actually redefines everything.

# The Ebb and Flow of Time and Tide

*A Short Play Based on "Grains and Seeds"*

Characters:

- **GELSOMINA** – A young widow, mother, and painter
- **SPIRIT OF ADAM** – Selena's late husband. His character is only visible to the readers and audience, not to the characters of the play.
- **SELENA** – Gelsomina's ten-year-old daughter

Setting:

- **Gelsomina's Cottage**
- **Brighton Beach**
- *The sunsets blending into the turquoise on the horizon* act as a life-changing event in the play.

Scene 1: Gelsomina's Cottage
*Lights up on* **GELSOMINA**, *standing barefoot near the edge of her balcony. A blurring cacophony plays in the background.*
**GELSOMINA**
*(softly crying)*
What life? I don't want this life, I am drowning… It feels like the end of the world. Each moment of my life tangled up in harsh reality, scattered like spilled seeds.
**SPIRIT OF ADAM**
*(audible only to audience, inaudible to the characters)*
But you have to let me go. Only then will you be at peace.
**SELENA**
*(wiping her mom's tears)*

Momma, why are you crying? Please don't cry, Momma...
I will be a good girl.

**SPIRIT OF ADAM**

That's my girl...

**SELENA**

So, where are we going to scatter Dad's ashes? Today
marks one year since his death anniversary.

**GELSOMINA**

Brighton Beach.

**SELENA**

What's so special about that beach, Momma?

**GELSOMINA**

Well, this is the very beach where your dad proposed
to me for the first time. This place holds many fond
memories.

*Reminiscing about old times makes Gelsomina emotional again,
but she hopes that maybe a change of place for a few days will be
good for both her and her daughter.*

Scene 2: Brighton Beach

*Lights up on* **GELSOMINA**, *standing barefoot near the edge of
the waves. She stares out at the horizon, painted in hues of pink,
red, and yellow. The sound of waves plays as background music.*
**SELENA** *enters the stage from left.*

**SELENA**

*(excitedly)*

Momma, will you be making sandcastles with me? And
will we be going scuba diving?

*Gelsomina nods her head in approval and continues to gaze at
the waves. With each wave hitting the shore and snatching away
the remnants of the past, Gelsomina realizes how the paths of
one's steadfast hopes are erased by the ebb and flow of tides.*

**GELSOMINA**
*(quietly to herself)*
Such is life. It's hard, it's complex, but we have to go on,
enduring the relentless ebb of days, searching for the
missing pieces of our jigsaw puzzle.
**SPIRIT OF ADAM**
*(audible only to audience)*
Finally, you are understanding. Paint again, love...
Painting will set you free.
**SELENA**
*(reminiscing her father's words)*
Momma, look! The tides are swallowing the sands. Can
you paint this? It's such a beautiful sight... you know,
Dada once told me when the grains of sand dissolve in the
sea, they signal new beginnings.
**SPIRIT OF ADAM**
*(emotional)*
I am proud of you, my child. You remember my words;
my heart fills with joy.
**GELSOMINA**
Yes, new traces emerge from the churn of life. In the void
of what's lost, subtle connections appear.
**SELENA**
I don't understand what you mean. This is sheer poetic
language... you're talking like Dada.
**GELSOMINA**
You will understand the meaning of this in due time.
**SPIRIT OF ADAM** *(laughing heartily, audible only to audience)*
They remember every bit of me—my words, my favorite
place. I don't know how things are going to turn out
for both of them, but Selena is there to take care of her
mother. I have no more worries. I can peacefully leave this
place now.

*Gelsomina and Selena scatter Adam's ashes. As tears roll down Gelsomina's cheeks, Selena once again wipes her tears.*

Scene 3: New Beginnings
*The sun begins to set, casting golden light over the stage.*
*GELSOMINA stands, brushing the sand off her hands. She looks out at the waves, her expression lighter.*
**GELSOMINA**
My heart doesn't feel heavy anymore.
**SELENA**
*(excited)*
If you are feeling better, Momma, then let's go scuba diving.
**GELSOMINA**
Not a bad idea, but let's do it tomorrow. For now, let's build our sandcastle.
**SELENA**
*(upset)*
Momma, the waves are breaking our castle.
**GELSOMINA**
Remember your dad's words: every dissolved grain of sand marks a fresh beginning. We will build a new castle again.
*Gelsomina witnesses the sunset blending into the horizon. She doesn't feel mad anymore; rather, she feels calm.*
**GELSOMINA**
*(monologue)*
My heart feels lighter. The tidal currents, glazed in crimson hues of sunset, echo my unmet aspirations of being a painter. I want to paint... I am going to paint again. It's my escape from this tangible world; it's my medium of expression.

**SELENA**
*(curious)*
What are you going to paint, Momma?
**GELSOMINA**
Let that be a surprise for now.
*Gelsomina realizes that going on this trip is one of the best decisions of her life.*
**GELSOMINA**
*(monologue)*
Time is a kaleidoscope of change, and everything or everyone is temporal or temporary in this mortal world. Only death and change are constant, and it's change that redefines everything.

**End of Play**

# The Forked Path

Our journey winds through alleys both straight and bent,
Each choice a turning point I embrace,
Though some paths lead us far from our intent,
They shape our hearts, our thoughts, our inner space.

A wrong turn taken may seem like a loss,
Yet landscapes viewed, and lessons learned anew,
Bring value to the journey, not the cost,
In winding ways, I find our purpose true.

For even when I wander, lost in night,
The dawn will break, revealing all I gained,
The less-traveled routes often bring the light,
To show the wisdom from the steps I've trained.

So fear not errant paths that life may show,
For every route leads to the shack I know.

# The Shack at the End of the Path
*A Short Story Based on "The Forked Path"*

The forest stretched endlessly before her eyes, like an endless maze of entwined paths. Disrupted patterns were drawn on the ground as the sunlight peeked through the thick canopy above. A years-old map with shredded edges was in her hands. Although the map was just like a puzzle to solve, like the routes themselves, it helped with little signs of her desired place due to its almost faded markings and lines, which looked mysterious enough.

As she started walking, her feet began to give up, causing pain as time turned from one hour to a few. Every fork ahead of her demanded a decision she had yet to make. The world surrounding her was quiet enough to hear the irregular rustle of leaves and the distant chirping of birds. With every decision, her doubt merged. Her mind dealt with questions like, "What if I choose the wrong path?" and "What if I am moving away from my goal, my destination?"

She had taken the right one from the first fork—a straight yet narrow path that seemed quite safe and trustable. The path later led her to a relatively calm field with wildflowers spotted throughout. Their vibrant nature gifted her a brief escape from the real-time uncertainty. Devouring the moment, she stood there and inhaled the sweet air of the surroundings before moving on.

But to her surprise, the second fork seemed to be more challenging. This time, the right path seemed rough and had a rocky structure, while the left path had a sharp curve leading to unknown darkness among the trees, resulting in a difficult climb. At first, she hesitated before taking the left, curved path, not knowing the result. Already, the right path with its unknown darkness had been intimidating her, but surprisingly, the darkness had its own beauty. It unfolded with a beautiful tiny stream over glossy moss above stones, its water cool and mirror-like clear. To drink from it, she stood there and tasted the heavenly pure water, which gave her the strength to walk ahead.

At the third fork, Clara sat on a fallen log, quietly gazing ahead, which displayed another tough choice to make. The left path looked like some tunnel with overgrown bushes, but the right one had footsteps. Unlike the previous ones, this time, Clara chose what appealed to her more—the left one—and the difficult one. She felt the left path contained more learnings and explorations for her.

Amidst her thoughts, an elderly man with a walking stick interrupted her. His beard shone just like the sunrays when they are reflected over the water streams. He smiled with warmth as he stepped forward, his eyes sparkling with wisdom.

"Are you lost, my child?" he asked gently.

Clara first hesitated but then nodded firmly, saying, "I am confused and don't know which path to choose."

While chuckling, the old man tapped his stick on the ground. "That's what makes this beautiful, isn't it? Because each path will end up teaching you something meaningful. It's not where you are going; it's about what you are going to learn throughout the journey."

She looked at the man and asked, "But what if my decision is wrong? What if I simply waste my decision on something that won't lead me anywhere?"

The man listened to her intently and answered, "You know, even a wrong path has its own worth. A wrong path can lead you to somewhere or something which you otherwise wouldn't have witnessed or learned. And who are we to say, 'What's wrong?' Every step builds us, even when you don't realize."

Clara turned and observed the left path once again and spoke, "That overgrown path seems difficult and risky."

The old man replied, understanding her worry. "These are some of the best journeys, you know. But now, you only decide."

With that, he adjusted his hat and started walking towards his worn path. Clara watched him until he disappeared from her sight, but his words still echoed in her mind.

She got up from the log and took a long breath before stepping onto the overgrown path. At first, she stumbled upon the rough ground and the side branches of the overgrown trees, but later, she slowly started to appreciate the beauty of the chaos she was in. She admired how the sun peeked through the branches, how the thick moss spread over the forest bed, and how the echo of a distant waterfall was tickling her ears.

Although her path was quite difficult, it had purpose and value. Sometimes, she questioned herself and her choices when she couldn't see her way, but she still didn't give up and closely held onto the old man's words that she was meant to be here.

It was almost evening when she exited the forest and finally stood in front of a tiny shack with worn yet solid wooden walls. A warm glow of a flame flickered from the windows, and smoke escaped from the chimney. It was a straightforward and modest path, but to Clara, it marked the end of a long and fruitful journey.

As she got closer, the door creaked open, and she realized upon her own journey that the hut was not just a hut but a reflection of all the choices she made throughout this journey. The journey had been worthwhile despite all its detours.

Because now morning had arrived, and she could see everything she had gained throughout the journey, even when she was roaming, lost in the night, in the dark. She finally realized what the old man had said: every path leads to the shack we know.

# Journey of the Forked Path

*A Short Play Based on "The Forked Path"*

Characters:

- **CLARA** – A young woman who is searching for the right direction in her life.
- **THE OLD MAN** – A wise traveler who gives advice, guidance, and perspective.
- **VOICE OF THE PATH** – A symbolic presence representing Clara's inner thoughts and the wisdom of the journey itself.
- **STEVE** – Clara's neighbor.

Setting:

- **Gelsomina's Cottage**
- **Brighton Beach**
- *The sunsets blending into the horizon* act as life-changing events in the play.
- **A dense forest with puzzled paths**, illuminated by flickering sunlight. The forest consists of many trails that emerge from the stage; some are weary, and some are overgrown. A small, rustic shack can be seen at a distance when the play concludes.

Scene 1: The First Fork

*Lights up on **CLARA**, standing at a trail fork. Her frown indicates her annoyance as she holds an old and battered map. The surroundings are filled with birds chirping and the rustling of leaves. The **VOICE OF THE PATH** resonates Clara's thoughts.*

**VOICE OF THE PATH**

Our journey winds through alleys both straight and bent,
Each choice a turning point I embrace.

**CLARA**

*(her eyes switching between the two paths)*

Why does it feel like whatever I choose can change everything? What if I make a wrong decision?

*She hesitates at first but then proceeds to take the right path, which is straight but weary. As she walks more, the light brightens, unveiling a breathtaking field full of wildflowers. Clara stands and smiles, absorbing the beauty through her eyes.*

**CLARA**

Maybe I did choose the right one. But then again, the Voice of the Path spoke...

**VOICE OF THE PATH**

Though some paths lead us far from our intent,
They shape our hearts, our thoughts, our inner space.

Scene 2: The Second Fork

*Clara reaches the next fork. Here, the left path takes a sharp turn that leads to something dark and rough, making her indecisive.*

**VOICE OF THE PATH**

A wrong turn taken may seem like a loss,
Yet landscapes viewed, and lessons learned anew...

**CLARA**

*(pauses)*

That's very easy to say, but doing it is difficult.

*The **THE OLD MAN** enters with his walking stick. He smiles at Clara warmly.*

**THE OLD MAN**

Are you lost?

**CLARA**

I don't like to admit it, but yes, unfortunately.

**THE OLD MAN**
Great, because if you are lost, that means you are exploring.
**CLARA**
But what will I do if I choose the wrong path?
**THE OLD MAN**
*(chuckles)*
There are no 'wrong paths,' as every path teaches a unique lesson. Every turn is a journey and an experience.
*He points toward the left path with the sharp turn.*
**CLARA**
But that one looks risky.
**THE OLD MAN**
Sometimes, the risky ones lead you to something fruitful.
*The Old Man adjusts his hat and continues walking. Clara watches him go until he disappears into the shadows, then takes a deep breath before choosing the left, shadowed path.*

Scene 3: The Third Fork
*The stage darkens as **CLARA** explores the overgrown third path. Overgrown branches poke at her, and the rough ground makes her steps messy. But she doesn't give up, believing in the Old Man's words. As she walks further, she notices a small stream with glossy moss. She kneels to drink, surprised by the beauty.*
**VOICE OF THE PATH**
In winding ways, I find our purpose true.
**VOICE OF THE PATH**
For even when I wander, lost in night,
The dawn will break, revealing all I gained.
*Clara's lips curl into a smile as her confidence grows. She continues walking, watching the light increase more and more.*

## Scene 4: The Little Shack Appears

*With the forest welcoming evening, Clara finally discovers a small shack as she exits the shadowed path. She sees smoke exiting from the chimney of the shack.*

**CLARA**

*(amused)*

Okay, so this is where my journey ends.

*The **THE OLD MAN** appears again, standing near the shack. He smiles at Clara as she approaches.*

**THE OLD MAN**

No, this is not the end, my child, but the beginning of another extraordinary chapter. Every path you chose led you here.

**CLARA**

You know, I was so confused and afraid of making these choices at first.

**THE OLD MAN**

But then, you made them successfully. You are now smarter, stronger, and prepared for whatever comes next because you faced the uncertainty.

**VOICE OF THE PATH**

*(thoughtfully)*

The less-traveled routes often bring the light,

To show the wisdom from the steps I've trained.

*The Old Man nods and points to the shack.*

**THE OLD MAN**

Go inside. Although your journey is still not over, for now, you have earned this. You deserve a rest.

*Clara walks toward the shack, feeling fully relaxed and calm. The **VOICE OF THE PATH** delivers its final lines as she enters.*

**VOICE OF THE PATH**
So fear not errant paths that life may show,
For every route leads to the shack I know.
*Clara enters. The light from within showcases on the stage. The
Old Man slowly disappears, and the sound of the path fades,
leaving only a peaceful stillness.*

## End of Play

# The Fire and the Flame

The fire's glow is a warm embrace?
a beacon in the cold.
But step closer
closer
too close—
and feel the searing sting

Some simmer gently, softly,
offering a constant, soothing warmth, popping
like a pot of boiling water

But others burn with fierce intensity—
too much to bear.

allure of their flame
promises connection and comfort.

Scorching, burning
leaving marks that time will never heal.

The boundary between warmth and woe
is fragile, easily crossed.

What once was comfort
turns to pain, the glow to burn.

In a tiny apartment
on East 9th Street, the fireplace,
with its ornate cast iron surround from a bygone era,
flickers invitingly.

The soft crackle of burning oak logs,
bought from the hardware store on 14th Street,
fills the room.

The scent of smoke
mingles with the aroma of fresh coffee
brewing in a vintage Bialetti on the stove.

But as you inch closer,
the heat becomes unbearable.
A spark jumps, landing on the edge of a faded Persian rug,
singeing the delicate fibers.

The mantle, cluttered with Polaroids, candles,
and an old brass clock from a thrift store on 23rd,
now radiates an intense heat.

# The Duality of the Fire

*A Short Story Based on "The Fire and the Flame"*

The tiny flat on East 9th Street was an amalgamation of both charm and chaos. With intricate scrollwork and tarnished brass pieces that reflected years of stories, there stood an elaborate cast-iron fireplace in the center—a history itself from a bygone period. As the December air howled outside, the fire sizzled warmly tonight, creating a layer of flickering shadows on the walls.

Evelyn sat on the floor, cross-legged, her hand wrapping around a steamy cup of coffee brewed from her vintage Bialetti. The aroma of the coffee spread widely, mingling with the woody smell from the burning oak logs she had brought home from the 14th Street hardware shop. It was like a ritual to her that she treasured—making coffee for herself while the warm glow of the fire illuminated the whole room, allowing her to finally enjoy the warmth that countered the city's cold nature.

The mantle above the fireplace showcased little memories and trinkets scattered all over, including an old brass clock that she had once found at the 23rd Street thrift shop. It also had various Polaroids pinned in an irregular pattern and half-burned candles. Although the place looked disoriented, mirroring Evelyn's existence, every element had a home.

The comfort of the warm glow gifted her solace and company in her solitude. She often, from time to time, mesmerized herself by the flames and found herself hypnotized by them. The way they popped and cracked like a pot of boiling water had a soothing effect. But as she drew closer due to the captivating effect, a sudden spark appeared and leapt from the firebox, falling on the edge of her Persian rug. In protest, the singed fibers curled up, forming a faint scar.

Evelyn, taking a moist cloth, smothered the area. Gazing deeply at the burned edge, she realized how easily the warmth could turn into something dangerous. She exhaled, put the piece of cloth down, and returned to her place. But now, the moment had altered completely. To her, the once comfortable fire had now changed into something fierce.

She realized that every relationship she had gone through was a fire of its own right. Some had simmered slowly, giving the required warmth, but some burned too deeply, leaving her with scars. She realized that the line dividing pain and comfort is very thin, just like a thread.

Evelyn found herself thinking of Edward, the man with whom she used to live in this apartment. Everything in its path had been consumed by the fierce fire that their love carried. Initially, the heat was a source of excitement, like a beacon that promised comfort and connection. But slowly, it became blazing, leaving her burned and scorched in ways that she is still coping with. She had now moved away from the glow that once lured her as it became unbearable.

She reached out for one Polaroid kept over the mantle. It was the photo of her and Edward, their first winter together at the apartment with snow-covered Central Park behind them. They were smiling, wrapped in coats and scarves together. She put the photo back after tracing its edges once again.

The fire crackled louder this time, as if to remind her of its presence. She moved away from it to keep herself safe. Although the place was quite warm and comfortable, it now carried duality. Sometimes it was comforting and sometimes destructive. Until it was crossed, the line between the two was very thin and nearly unrecognizable.

As she sipped her coffee, the bitter warmth helped her stay grounded. She watched the flames, no longer hypnotized by them, but more reflective now. She recalled the lessons she learned through the burning rug and the small blackened scar. Just like fire, life was also unpredictable; it could offer both warmth and woe. Embracing it meant accepting the risk, knowing that even the most calming flame can turn into a burn. Knowing that even the most calming glow could turn into a burn, embracing it meant taking the chance.

As the night deepened, Evelyn stood and carefully repositioned the fire, adding more wood logs into it and making sure the screen was in place. With the brass clock ticking behind her, Evelyn blew out the candles, adjusted the Polaroids on the mantle. She no longer leaned toward the burning fire as she did in the past, which still burned and illuminated the room.

Rather, she sat distant, grabbing her coffee and respectfully watching the flames. She would maintain her distance as the warmth she received was adequate. She realized that some fires are not meant to be embraced but rather admired. She sat far away, holding her coffee and respectfully observing the flames. She would maintain her limits, and the warmth they provided was sufficient. She understood that some fires were not to be embraced but rather admired.

# The Lessons of the Fire

*A Short Play Based on "The Fire and the Flame"*

**Characters:**

- **EVELYN** – A woman who is living alone but struggles with her memories and boundaries.
- **EDWARD** – Evelyn's ex-partner who only appears through Evelyn's Polaroids and flashbacks.
- **VOICE OF THE FLAME** – A symbolic representation of the fire, embodying its lessons, danger, and fascination.
- **SELENA** – Evelyn's ten-year-old daughter.

**Setting:**

- **Evelyn's Apartment on East 9th Street**
- **Brighton Beach**
- *A dense forest with puzzled paths, illuminated by flickering light from sunrays. The forest consists of many trails that emerge from the stage; some are weary, and some are overgrown. A small, rustic shack can be seen at a distance when the play concludes.*
- **Neon lights** act as a recurrent motif in the play, symbolizing transitions and emotional states.

Scene 1: The Coffee and the Warm Glow

*Lights up on* **EVELYN**, *standing barefoot near the edge of her balcony. A blurring cacophony plays in the background. The cast-iron fireplace stands at the center, casting flickering shadows. Over the mantle, a bronze clock, Polaroids, and candles are scattered all over. On the floor near the fireplace is a Persian rug.*

**EVELYN**
(softly crying)
What life? I don't want this life. I am drowning... It feels
like the end of the world. Each moment of my life tangled
up in harsh reality, scattered like spilled seeds.
**VOICE OF THE FLAME**
(audible only to audience, inaudible to the characters)
But you have to let me go. Only then will you be at peace.
**SELENA**
(wiping her mom's tears)
Momma, why are you crying? Please don't cry, Momma...
I will be a good girl.
**VOICE OF THE FLAME**
That's my girl...
**SELENA**
So, where are we going to scatter Dad's ashes? Today
marks one year since his death anniversary.
**EVELYN**
Brighton Beach.
**SELENA**
What's so special about that beach, Momma?
**EVELYN**
Well, this is the very beach where your dad proposed to me
for the first time. This place holds many fond memories.
*Reminiscing about old times makes Evelyn emotional again,*
*but she hopes that maybe a change of place for a few days will be*
*good for both her and her daughter.*

Scene 2: Brighton Beach
*Lights up on* **EVELYN**, *standing barefoot near the edge of the*
*waves. She stares out at the horizon, painted in hues of pink,*
*red, and yellow. The sound of waves plays as background music.*
**SELENA** *enters the stage from left.*

**SELENA**
*(excitedly)*
Momma, will you be making sandcastles with me? And will we be going scuba diving?
*Evelyn nods her head in approval and continues to gaze at the waves. With each wave hitting the shore and snatching away the remnants of the past, Evelyn realizes how the paths of one's steadfast hopes are erased by the ebb and flow of tides.*

**EVELYN**
*(quietly to herself)*
Such is life. It's hard, it's complex, but we have to go on, enduring the relentless ebb of days, searching for the missing pieces of our jigsaw puzzle.

**VOICE OF THE FLAME**
*(audible only to audience)*
Finally, you are understanding. Paint again, love... Painting will set you free.

**SELENA**
*(reminiscing her father's words)*
Momma, look! The tides are swallowing the sands. Can you paint this? It's such a beautiful sight... You know, Dada once told me when the grains of sand dissolve in the sea, they signal new beginnings.

**VOICE OF THE FLAME**
*(emotional, audible only to audience)*
I am proud of you, my child. You remember my words; my heart fills with joy.

**EVELYN**
Yes, new traces emerge from the churn of life. In the void of what's lost, subtle connections appear.

**SELENA**
I don't understand what you mean. This is sheer poetic language... You're talking like Dada.

**EVELYN**

You will understand the meaning of this in due time.

**VOICE OF THE FLAME**

*(laughing heartily, audible only to audience)*

They remember every bit of me—my words, my favorite place. I don't know how things are going to turn out for both of you, but Selena is there to take care of her mother. I have no more worries. I can peacefully leave this place now.

*Evelyn and Selena scatter Adam's ashes. As tears roll down Evelyn's cheeks, Selena once again wipes her tears.*

Scene 3: New Beginnings

*The sun begins to set, casting golden light over the stage.*
*EVELYN stands, brushing the sand off her hands. She looks out at the waves, her expression lighter.*

**EVELYN**

My heart doesn't feel heavy anymore.

**SELENA**

*(excited)*

If you are feeling better, Momma, then let's go scuba diving.

**EVELYN**

Not a bad idea, but let's do it tomorrow. For now, let's build our sandcastle.

**SELENA**

*(upset)*

Momma, the waves are breaking our castle.

**EVELYN**

Remember your dad's words: every dissolved grain of sand marks a fresh beginning. We will build a new castle again.

*Evelyn witnesses the sunset blending into the horizon. She doesn't feel mad anymore; rather, she feels calm.*

**EVELYN**

*(monologue)*

My heart feels lighter. The tidal currents, glazed in crimson hues of sunset, echo my unmet aspirations of being a painter. I want to paint... I am going to paint again. It's my escape from this tangible world; it's my medium of expression.

**SELENA**

*(curious)*

What are you going to paint, Momma?

**EVELYN**

Let that be a surprise for now.

*Evelyn realizes that going on this trip is one of the best decisions of her life.*

**EVELYN**

*(monologue)*

Time is a kaleidoscope of change, and everything or everyone is temporal or temporary in this mortal world. Only death and change are constant, and it's change that redefines everything.

**End of Play**

## Black Eagle Books

www.blackeaglebooks.org
info@blackeaglebooks.org

Black Eagle Books, an independent publisher, was founded as a nonprofit organization in April, 2019. It is our mission to connect and engage the Indian diaspora and the world at large with the best of works of world literature published on a collaborative platform, with special emphasis on foregrounding Contemporary Classics and New Writing.